Hiccup Harry

Chris Powling
and
Scoular Anderson

Collins

This edition produced for The Book People Ltd
Hall Wood Avenue, Haydock
St Helens WA11 9UL

Published by Young Lions in 1988
and reprinted by Collins in 1995

10

ISBN 0-00-763091-3

Collins an imprint of
HarperCollins*Publishers* Ltd,
77-85 Fulham Palace Road
Hammersmith, London W6 8JB.

Text copyright © Chris Powling 1988
Illustrations copyright © Scoular Anderson

Printed and bound in Great Britain by
Omnia Books Limited, Glasgow

Do you know what a hiccup is?

This is the story of the worst hiccups I ever had. Every kid in my school had to stop work because of them.

It happened when I was {HIC!} years old! Six years old, I mean.

The hiccups began when we were sitting cross-legged on the carpet in the book corner.

Miss Hobbs was calling the register.

'He's got hiccups, Miss,' said Sharon.
'I can hear that,' said Miss Hobbs.
'Now settle down, please. It's not
that funny. Remember what we
said yesterday about
helping Harry
behave himself?
I promised his
Mum he'd have
a perfect day,
today.
Okay, Harry?'

CACTUS
TABLE

Miss Hobbs gave me one of her
spikey looks. She thought I was
mucking about again.
'Pull yourself together, Harry,'
she snapped.

'I don't want to hear any more of
those hiccups. You can control them
if you want to.'

I didn't dare ask her how.

So when it was our turn in the playhouse I asked Tracey instead.

'It's easy-peasy,' she whispered.
'You can make hiccups go away
by singing a song, Harry.
My Dad told me.'

'A song?' I said. 'What kind of 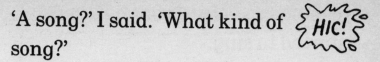 song?'
'It doesn't matter. Any song will do.'

This sounded daft to me but I hadn't got a better idea.

Keeping my voice as low as I could
I started to sing.

This made Tracey giggle.

'Shut up!' I hissed.
'But you're so funny, Harry.'

By now Bernard and Sharon were
giggling as well.

If I was quick, though, I might stop
the hiccups before Miss Hobbs
heard me.

All the HIC! horses

And all the HIC! men

Couldn't put HIC together again.

Half the class had the giggles by this time.

They were crowding round the playhouse to hear my singing.

Or maybe they wanted to hear my
hiccups. Whichever it was they were

With a

CRASH!

a

CLATTER

and the loudest

Bonkety Bonk!

you ever heard,

the playhouse collapsed on top of
Tracey and me.

Miss Hobbs wasn't very pleased.

When at last

she'd sorted it all out

she fixed me with another of
those looks.
'I might have known you'd be at the
bottom of this, Harry. What have
you got to say for yourself?'

Guess what I said?

You're right.

Which is why I was sent to the medical room.

A long, cool glass of water?

Terrif. . .   . . .HIC!

But where was the long, cool glass

HIC! to put the water in?

It was ages before I found one.

It stood on top of Mrs Frisby's big
cupboard just where I couldn't
HIC! reach it.

Yes, I know I should have waited for
Mrs Frisby.

She's our school help and she's never
out of the medical room for long.

I was in a  hurry, though.
So I opened the cupboard doors.
And I stepped up on the bottom shelf.

And I stepped up on the second shelf.

And I stepped up on the third shelf.

Now, if I stretched out my hand
I could reach the glass.

Why was it sliding towards me,
though?

The hiccup seemed to tip the cupboard forwards as I fell backwards.

I hit the ground in a shower of books

and tins and boxes

and old registers

and lost property

and first-aid stuff.

How the cupboard itself missed me I
don't know. It was the only thing
that did miss.

I felt as if I'd been buried under a jumble sale. And all because of my hiccup! It wasn't fair. Mrs Frisby was bound to think it was me who made the mess.

'Better get out of here, Harry,' I told myself.

So I scuttled into the corridor.

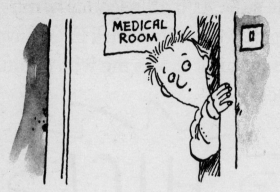

I was halfway back to class when a big kid from the juniors stopped me.

'What's the rush, littlie?' he asked.

39

Normally I'd be too shy to talk to a junior but this one looked so friendly I told him everything.

He liked the bit about the playhouse especially.
'That's great,' he laughed. 'You're the funniest littlie I ever met.'

43

When the junior had gone I looked along the corridor. Where was there room for a handstand? One side of the corridor was window

and the other side was covered with
paintings and drawings.

Except one place.

Here was a bit of wall where a red bucket hung on a hook beside a small, glass box.

'That'll do, HIC!' I said. 'I'd better make this my best handstand ever.'

One

two

three

HICCUP!

went my left
heel as it hit
the red bucket.

TINKLE TINKLE!

went my right
heel as it hit the
small, glass box.

Then . . .

DINGA — DINGA
DINGA — DINGA
DINGA
DINGA — DINGA — DINGA
DINGA — DINGA
DINGA — DINGA
DINGA — DINGA

I heard doors opening, the shuffle of feet and the sound of teachers getting kids into straight, quiet lines. It was fire-drill.

Everybody would stay out in the playground till our headteacher Mrs Cadett had made sure the school was empty.

Somebody had rung the alarm-bell, you see.

No, not *someone*.

Suddenly I realised what had happened. My hiccup had started the fire-bell when my handstand broke the glass in the small box!

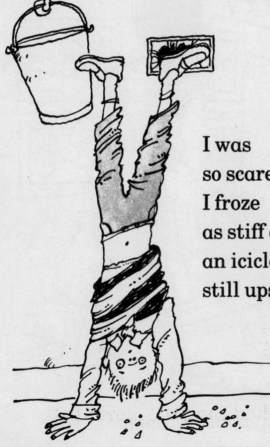

I was
so scared
I froze
as stiff as
an icicle,
still upside down.

The school was silent now. Even the
dinga-dinga-dinga-dinga had
stopped. I heard footsteps coming
towards me. I didn't dare move. I
knew straightaway who it was.

said Mrs Cadett.
I felt her eyes shift from me to the
broken glass and back again.

When Mrs Cadett is happy she has a face like a smiley lion. Now, seen from the bottom end of a handstand, she seemed to me like a growly lion.

'Wait for me in my room, Harry,'
she said. 'I'd better get everyone
back into school again. I expect they
think the school is burning down.'
In Mrs Cadett's room I waited

and waited.

At last she came.
By now I was so terrified I kept my
eyes on the carpet in front of her desk.

'Harry,' she said. 'I've been talking
to Miss Hobbs and Mrs Frisby.
You've been causing quite a
commotion this morning.'

'It wasn't my fault,' I wailed.
'Honestly, it wasn't. My hiccups
knocked over the playhouse. And
my hiccups upset Mrs Frisby's
cupboard. And it was my hiccups
that rang the fire-bell.'

'Your hiccups did all that? They
must be pretty special hiccups.
May I hear one?'
'Okay,' I said.

I stood there.

'Go on, Harry,' said Mrs Cadett.

Still I stood there.

You can probably guess what my problem was. My hiccups had vanished.

Yes, *vanished*.

I couldn't believe it. Just when I needed them, they'd gone.

It was as if I'd never had a hiccup in my life – as if I'd been telling fibs about everything. What would Mrs Cadett do to me now?

Suddenly . . .

Not me, no. The hiccup had come
from Mrs Cadett. When I looked up
I saw a huge grin on her face.

'That was a fake hiccup, Harry,' she
said. 'But I've had the real hiccups
all morning – till the fire-bell gave
me such a fright they disappeared.'

'That's when my hiccups went!' I said.

'Tell me about them,' she grinned.
'And I'll tell you about mine.'
Then she gave me a wink. I'd forgotten
that Mrs Cadett could be a
laughing lion.

Of course I had to help with
the clearing up – and promise
never to go near the firebell again.

The best part, though, was when
Mum collected me from school
because Mrs Cadett got her to see
the funny side too. We joked about
it all the way home.

Mind you, Mum reckons the next time I have hiccups I'd better stay outside in our back garden. She doesn't want the house to fall down, she says.